Lenny
the Lucky Pup

HARMANEE

INDIA • SINGAPORE • MALAYSIA

ISBN 979-8-89929-945-2

LENNY THE LUCKY PUP

DEDICATION

I dedicate this book to my awesome Dad and Mum for helping rescue Lenny, and to my Auntie Raj; without her, we would never have met him.

I would also like to dedicate my first book to my grandparents, aunts, uncles, cousins, friends and teachers who have inspired and supported my creative imagination over the years – thank you.

And, of course, I can't forget my first pup, Skye. You were the best teacher, my first furry BFF, and you left us way too soon. Miss you always.

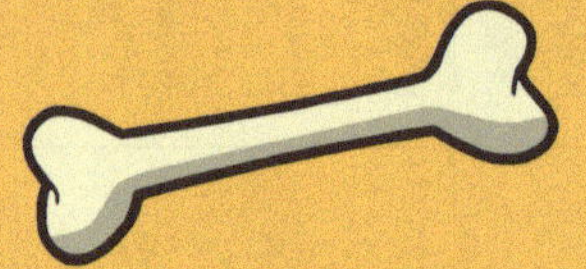

Lenny was a big, chocolate-brown dog with a white chest and paws. His eyes were this weird mix of yellow and green, and he always looked like he just heard someone say, "No more treats."

Lenny used to live in a house where nobody played with him.

No belly rubs, no snacks, no love —just nothing. If I were him, I would've packed a suitcase and left. But, you know, no thumbs.

Then one day, daddy, mummy and I went to meet him. He wagged his tail so hard I thought he might take off like a helicopter.

"We're taking you home, buddy," my daddy said, putting a super fluffy blanket in the car.

Lenny jumped in like, Finally!

My Uber is here.

9

At bedtime, Lenny curled up at my feet. "You're home now," I whispered.

He sighed like he'd just eaten a really good burger.

Our house was warm and full of hugs and snacks. But Lenny? Oh boy. He had no clue how to "sit" or "stay." Walking on a leash? Ha! More like a roller coaster.

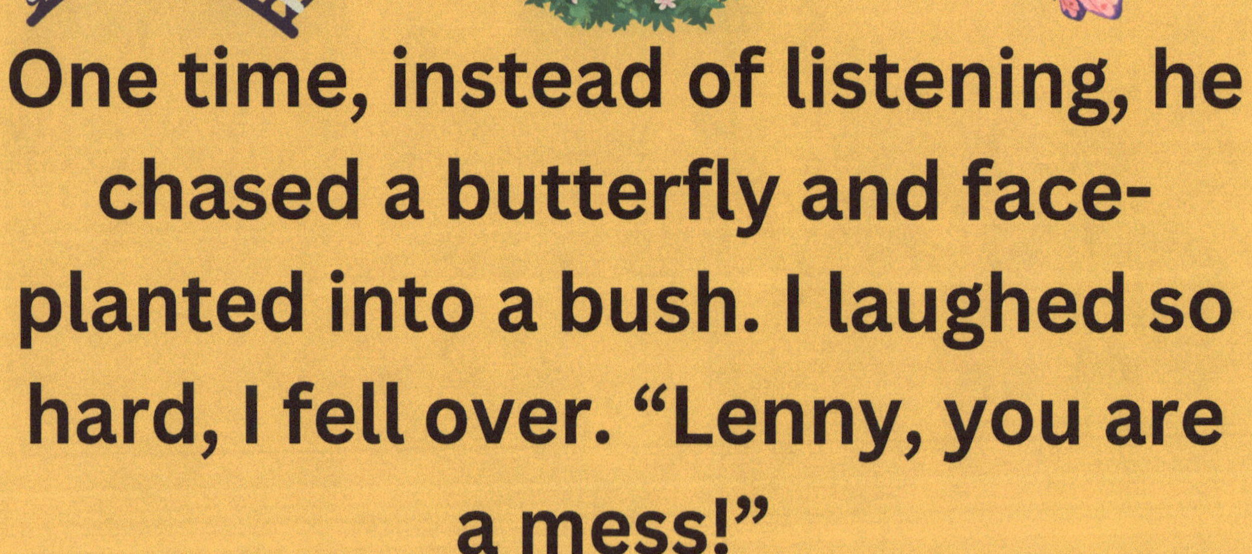

One time, instead of listening, he chased a butterfly and face-planted into a bush. I laughed so hard, I fell over. "Lenny, you are a mess!"

13

Daddy tried to teach him. "Sit, Lenny!" he said, holding a treat.

Lenny just stared at him like, Define 'sit.'

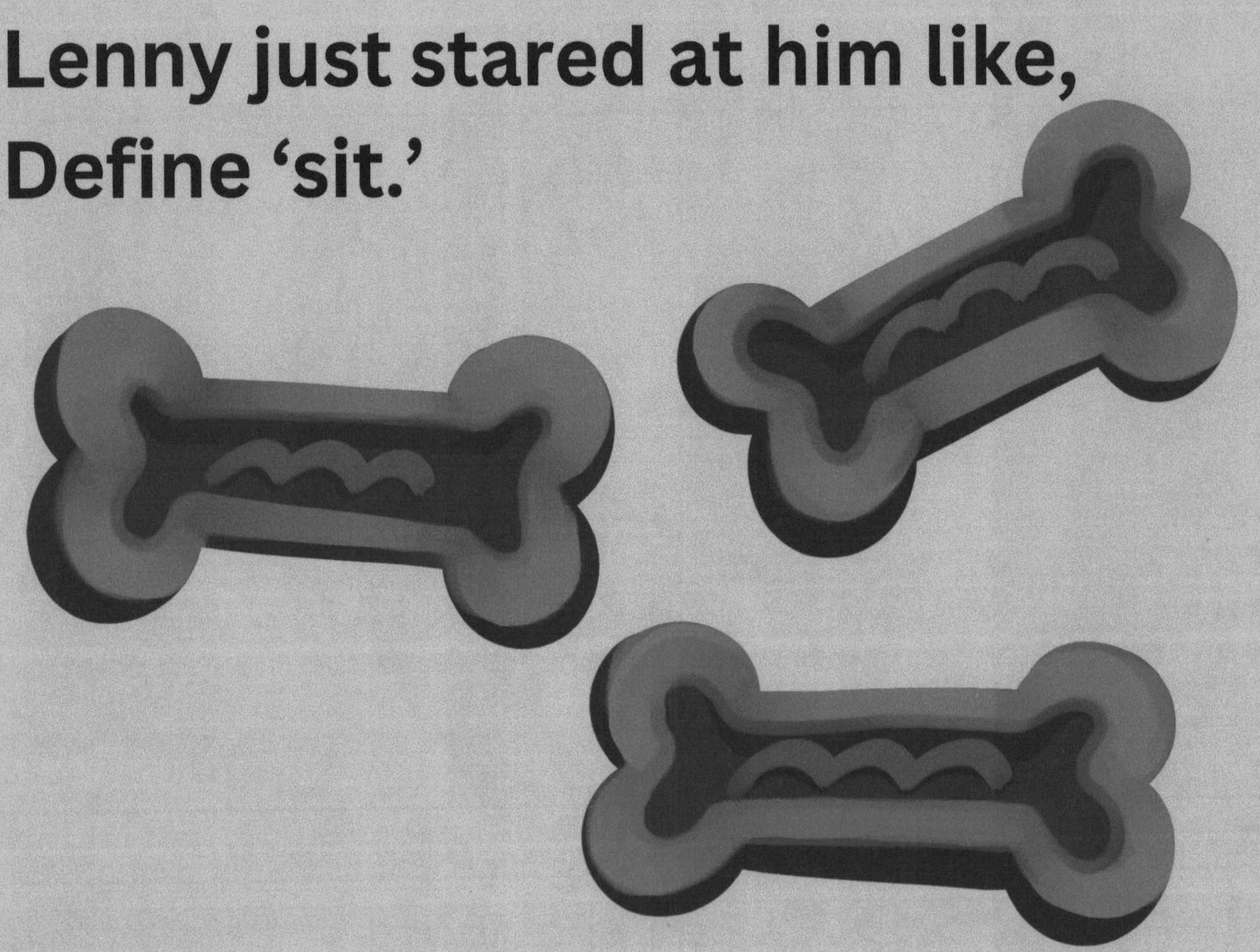

15

So I sat on the floor and said,
"Like this, Lenny!"

He tilted his head, then licked
my face. That was not the
assignment.

But then, BOOM. He plopped his butt down! "YES, Lenny! You're a genius!" Dad gave him the treat. I took credit.

Day by day, Lenny got smarter.
He learned to walk next to me instead of dragging me like a sled dog.

He waited for his dinner (most of the time). He even came when we called him! Miracles.

Sometimes, he got too excited and jumped up on people.

"Down, Lenny!" Daddy reminded him. But, honestly? Free hugs. I didn't mind!

My awesome cousin brother
Dillon loved coming to play and
cuddle Lenny, we all became
best friends!

One day at the park, another dog barked at me.

Lenny stepped right in front of me, wagging his tail but keeping an eye on Mr. Loudmouth

"It's okay, Lenny," I said. The big dog sniffed the air, decided we weren't worth the drama, and walked away. Lenny stood tall like a bodyguard.

My handsome furry bodyguard.

Lenny loved us, and we loved him. He wasn't just some dog we rescued,

He was part of our pack now!!!

We ran around the garden,
played hide-and-seek (he was
terrible at it), and snuggled on
the couch.

Lenny had hit the jackpot.

"I'm so proud of you, Lenny," Daddy said. "You've learned so much." Lenny wagged his tail like, Yeah, I know.

I giggled. "And he taught me something too, Daddy." "What's that?" Daddy asked. "That love and patience can change everything," I said, hugging Lenny tight.

And I swear, Lenny smiled.
Probably because he knew—he
was the luckiest pup in the world!

About the Author

Harmanee is a creative 9-year-old who has just written her very first book! When she isn't busy writing, she loves experimenting with fun slime projects and using her imagination. Most of all, she adores her best friend, Lenny.

Lenny is a sweet 5-year-old XL American Bully who now lives in London with his new family. He was rescued when he was two, and although he later became part of a banned breed in 2024—a very challenging time for everyone—his family was determined to keep him safe and loved.

Through her writing, Harmanee hopes to show that being a responsible dog owner means understanding a dog's behaviour and giving them the proper care and training.

Harmanee aims to inspire all children who own dogs, regardless of breed, to learn how to train them properly and treat them with the respect they deserve.

Thank you for reading, and we hope you enjoyed the book!